H.E. Manning

The Treatise on Purgatory

SALZWASSER
VERLAG

H.E. Manning

The Treatise on Purgatory

Reprint of the original, first published in 1858.

1st Edition 2023 | ISBN: 978-3-37515-522-3

Salzwasser Verlag is an imprint of Outlook Verlagsgesellschaft mbH.

Verlag (Publisher): Outlook Verlag GmbH, Zeilweg 44, 60439 Frankfurt, Deutschland
Vertretungsberechtigt (Authorized to represent): E. Roepke, Zeilweg 44, 60439 Frankfurt, Deutschland
Druck (Print): Books on Demand GmbH, In de Tarpen 42, 22848 Norderstedt, Deutschland

A TREATISE ON PURGATORY.

THE TREATISE ON PURGATORY

BY

ST. CATHERINE OF GENOA.

Translated from the original Italian.

WITH A PREFACE BY

THE VERY REV. H. E. MANNING, D.D.

PROVOST OF WESTMINSTER.

"In iis quæ de Purgatorio determinata non sunt ab Ecclesiâ standum est iis quæ sunt magis conformia dictis et revelationibus Sanctorum."—St. Thomas, in 4 sent. dist. 21, quæst. 1, a. 1; quoted by Bellarmine, lib. ii. c. vii. de Purg.

LONDON:

BURNS AND LAMBERT, 17 PORTMAN STREET,
AND 63 PATERNOSTER ROW.

1858.

PREFACE.

THE Treatise of St. Catherine of Genoa on Purgatory has never, it seems, been as yet rendered into English. The present translation, therefore, which is both faithful and excellent in language, will be most acceptable to those to whom this wonderful book has hitherto been closed.

Although our Lord, by His apostle, has forbidden to women the public ministry of teaching in His Church, He has nevertheless reserved for them a great and resplendent office in the edification of His mystical Body. The lights and inspirations bestowed upon them, according to the words of the prophet Joel,—" In the last days, saith the Lord, I will pour out of My Spirit upon all flesh, and your sons and your daughters shall prophesy ; . . . and upon My servants and upon My handmaidens I will pour out in those days of My Spirit,"—are among the prerogatives bestowed upon the Church by the day of Pentecost.   And their dignity is among the glories of the Mother of God, whose daughters and handmaids they are.

Two of the great festivals of the Catholic Church had their origin in the illumination of humble and unlearned women.   The Feast of Corpus Christi was the offspring of the devotion of the Blessed Juliana of Retinne; the Feast of the Sacred Heart of that of the Blessed Margaret Mary: to St. Catherine of Sienna our Lord vouchsafed the honour of calling back again the Sovereign Pontiff from the splendid banishment of Avignon to the throne of the Apostolic See; to St. Teresa the special gift of illumination, to teach the ways of union with Himself in prayer; to Blessed Angela of Foligno the eighteen degrees of compunction, and His own five poverties; and to St. Catherine of Genoa an insight and perception of the state of Purgatory, which seem like the utterances of one immersed in its expiation of love.

Benedict XIV. tells us, in his work on the Beatification and Canonisation of Saints, that the works of St. Catherine of Genoa were examined and approved by the theologians of Paris: intending, no doubt, the examination by the

Sorbonne in 1666, by direction of the Arch-
bishop of Paris; and again by the Sacred Con-
gregation in the cause of her canonisation.*
The source from which she drew the sweet and
consoling illumination set forth in the following
pages, on the mysterious sufferings and bliss of
purgatory, was a life of continued pain and of
ardent consuming love; of perpetual expiation,
and of absolute conformity to the will of God.
And of this she says: " This way of purgation
which I see in the souls in purgatory, I feel in
my own mind, chiefly in the last two years;
day by day I feel and see it more clearly. I
see my soul to be standing in the body as in a
purgatory conformed and like to the true purgatory. . . . All the things I have hitherto said
I see and touch : but I can find no fit words to
express as fully as I desire to say it; and what
I have said I feel to be working spiritually within
me, and therefore I have said it."†

The Saint was born in Genoa, in 1447, of
the family of Fieschi. Her parents married
her to Giuliano Adorno, of a noble Genoese
house. After his death she served the sick in
the Great Hospital, where her body, still per-

* Ben. XIV. de Beat. et Can. Sanct. lib. ii. c. xxvi. 2.
† Trattato del Purgatorio, c. xvii.

fect and visible, is venerated over the high altar
in the choir of the religious which is attached
to the wards, and looks down upon the ex-
ternal Church; and her memory is blessed
among the saints as the Seraph of Genoa.

H. E. M.

All Souls Day, 1858.

A

TREATISE ON PURGATORY.

The Saint shows how she understood Purgatory from the divine fire which she felt within herself, and in what manner the souls there are both happy and tormented.

CHAPTER I.

STATE OF THE SOULS IN PURGATORY, HOW THEY ARE FREE FROM ALL SELF-LOVE.

THIS holy soul, yet in the flesh, found herself placed in the purgatory of God's burning love, which consumed and purified her from whatever she had to purify, in order that after passing out of this life she might enter at once into the immediate presence of God her Beloved. By means of this furnace of love she understood how the souls of the faithful are placed in purgatory to get rid of all the rust and stain of sin that in this life was left unpurged. As she, plunged in the divine furnace of purifying love, was united to the object of her love,

B

and satisfied with all that He wrought in her, so she understood it to be with the souls in purgatory, and said :

The souls in purgatory, as far as I can understand the matter, cannot but choose to be there ; and this by God's ordinance, who has justly decreed it so. They cannot reflect within themselves and say, "I have done such and such sins, for which I deserve to be here ;" nor can they say, " Would that I had not done them, that now I might go to paradise ;" nor yet say, " That soul is going out before me ;" nor, " I shall go out before him." They can remember nothing of themselves or others, whether good or evil, which might increase the pain they ordinarily endure ; they are so completely satisfied with what God has ordained for them, that He should be doing all that pleases Him, and in the way it pleases Him, that they are incapable of thinking of themselves even in the midst of their greatest sufferings. They behold only the goodness of God, whose mercy is so great in bringing men to Himself, that they cannot see any thing that may affect them, whether good or bad ; if they could, they would not be in pure charity. They do not know that their sufferings are for the sake of their sins, nor can they keep in view the sins themselves ;* for in doing so there would be an act of imperfection, which could have no place where there can be no longer any possibility of actually sinning.

* See Appendix A.

Once, in passing out of this life, they perceive why they have their purgatory; but never afterwards, otherwise self would come in. Abiding, then, in charity, and not being able to deviate therefrom by any real defect, they have no will, no desire, nothing but the will of pure love : they are in that fire of purgatory by the appointment of God, which is all one with pure love ; and they cannot in any thing turn aside from it, because, as they can no more merit, so they can no more sin.

CHAPTER II.

THE JOY OF THE SOULS IN PURGATORY—THE SAINT SHOWS HOW THEY ARE EVER SEEING GOD MORE AND MORE—DIFFICULTY IN SPEAKING OF THEIR CONDITION.

I DO not believe it would be possible to find any joy comparable to that of a soul in purgatory, except the joy of the blessed in paradise,—a joy which goes on increasing day by day, as God more and more flows in upon the soul, which He does abundantly in proportion as every hindrance to His entrance is consumed away. The hindrance* is the rust of sin ; the fire consumes the rust, and thus the soul goes on laying itself open to the Divine inflowing.

It is as with a covered object. The object cannot respond to the rays of the sun, not because the sun ceases to shine,—for it shines without intermission,—but because the covering intervenes. Let the

* See Appendix B.

covering be destroyed, again the object will be exposed to the sun, and will answer to the rays which beat against it in proportion as the work of destruction advances. Thus the souls are covered by a rust—that is, sin—which is gradually consumed away by the fire of purgatory; the more it is consumed, the more they respond to God their true Sun; their happiness increases as the rust falls off, and lays them open to the Divine ray; and so their happiness grows greater as the impediment grows less, till the time is accomplished. The pain, however, does not diminish, but only the time of remaining in that pain. As far as their will is concerned, these souls cannot acknowledge the pain as such, so completely are they satisfied with the ordinance of God, so entirely is their will one with it in pure charity. On the other hand, they suffer a torment so extreme, that no tongue could describe it, no intellect could form the least idea of it, if God had not made it known by special grace; which idea, however, God's grace has shown my soul; but I cannot find words to express it with my tongue, yet the sight of it has never left my mind. I will describe it as I can: they will understand it whose intellect the Lord shall vouchsafe to open.

CHAPTER III.

SEPARATION FROM GOD IS THE GREATEST PUNISHMENT OF PURGATORY—WHEREIN PURGATORY DIFFERS FROM HELL.

ALL the pains of purgatory take their rise from sin, original or actual. God created the soul perfectly pure and free from every spot of sin, with a certain instinctive tendency to find its blessedness in Him. From this tendency it is drawn away by original sin, and still more by the addition of actual sin; and the farther off it gets, the more wicked it becomes, because it is less in conformity with God.

Things are good only so far as they participate in God. To irrational creatures God communicates Himself, without fail, as He wills, and as He has determined; to the rational soul more or less, according as He finds it purified from the impediment of sin; so that, when a soul is approaching to that state of first purity and innocence which it had when created, the instinctive desire of seeking happiness in God develops itself, and goes on increasing through the fire of love, which draws it to its end with such impetuosity and vehemence, that any obstacle seems intolerable, and the more clear its vision, the more extreme its pain.

Now because the souls in purgatory are without the guilt of sin, there is nothing to stand between God and them except the punishment which keeps them back, and prevents this instinct from attaining its perfection; and from their keenly perceiving of what moment it is to be hindered even in the least degree, and yet that justice most strictly demands a hindrance, there springs up within them a fire like that of hell. They have not the guilt of sin; and it is this latter which constitutes the malignant will of the damned, who are excluded from sharing in the goodness of God, and therefore remain in that hopeless malignity of will by which they oppose the will of God.

CHAPTER IV.

STATE OF THE SOULS THAT ARE IN HELL, AND THE DIFFERENCE THERE IS BETWEEN THEM AND THOSE IN PURGATORY—REFLECTIONS OF THE SAINT UPON THOSE WHO NEGLECT THEIR SALVATION.

FROM what has been said, it is clear that the guilt of sin consists in the perverse opposition of the will to the will of God, and that so long as the will continues thus evilly perverse the guilt will continue. For those, then, in hell, who have departed this life with an evil will, there is no remission of sin, neither can be, because there can be no more change of will. In passing out of this life the soul is fixed for good or evil, according to its deliberate purpose at the time; as it is written, "*Where I shall find thee* (that is, at the hour of death, with a will either to sin or sorry for sin and penitent), *there will I judge thee:*" and this judgment is final; because after death the will can never again be free, but must remain fixed in the condition in which it was found at the moment of death. The souls in hell having been found at the moment of death with a will to sin, have with them an infinite degree of guilt; and the punishment they suffer, though less than they deserve, is yet, so far as it exists, endless. But the souls in purgatory have only the punishment for sin, and not its guilt; for the guilt was effaced at the moment of death, in that they were found then deploring their sins and penitent for having offended the Divine Goodness: so their punishment has a limit, and goes on diminishing in duration as has been said.

O misery above every misery! and so much the greater because men in their blindness consider it so little.

The punishment of the damned is not, indeed, infinite in amount; for the sweet goodness of God sheds the rays of His mercy even in hell. A man who has died in mortal sin deserves a punishment infinite in pain and infinite in duration; but God in His mercy has made it infinite only in duration, and has limited the amount of pain. He might most justly have given them a far greater punishment than He has.

O how perilous is a sin committed through malice! for hardly does a man repent of it; and not repenting, his guilt remains, and will remain, so long as there is any affection for the sin committed, or any purpose of committing it afresh.

CHAPTER V.

THE PEACE AND JOY OF PURGATORY.

THE souls in purgatory having their wills perfectly conformed to the will of God, and hence partaking of His goodness, remain satisfied with their condition, which is one of entire freedom from the guilt of sin. For when they passed out of this life, penitent, with all their sins confessed and resolved to sin no more, God straightway pardoned them; and now they are as pure as when they were created; the rust of sin alone is left, and this they get rid of by the punishment of fire. Cleansed thus from all sin, and united in will to God, they see God clearly according to the degree of light He imparts to them; they are conscious too what a thing it is for them to enjoy God, that for this very end souls were created. Again, there is in them a conformity of will so uniting them to God, so drawing them to Him through that natural instinct whereby God is, as it were, bound up with the soul, that no description, no figure, no example can give a clear idea of it as it is actually felt and apprehended by inward consciousness; nevertheless I will mention something like it which suggests itself to me.

CHAPTER VI.

COMPARISON TO EXPLAIN THE IMPETUOSITY AND LOVE BY WHICH THE SOULS IN PURGATORY DESIRE TO ENJOY GOD.

LET us suppose that there existed in the world but one loaf of bread to satisfy the hunger of every creature, and that the mere sight of it could do this. In such a case a man, having naturally, if in good health, a desire for food, would find himself, so long as he was kept from dying or falling sick, getting more and more hungry; for his craving would continue undiminished,—he would know that the bread, and nothing but the bread, could satisfy him, and not being able to reach it, would remain in intolerable pain; the nearer he got to the bread without seeing it, the more ardently would he crave for it, and would direct himself wholly towards it, as being the only thing which could afford him relief; and if he were assured that he never could see the bread he would have within him a perfect hell, and become like the damned, who are cut off from all hope of ever seeing God their Saviour, who is the true Bread.

The souls in purgatory, on the other hand, hope to see that Bread, and satiate themselves to the full therewith; whence they hunger and suffer pain as great as will be their capacity of enjoying that Bread, which is Jesus Christ the true God, our Saviour and our Love.

CHAPTER VII.

THE WONDERFUL WISDOM OF GOD IN THE INVENTION OF PURGATORY AND HELL.

As the soul cleansed and purified finds no place wherein to rest but God, this being its end by creation, so the soul in a state of sin finds no place for it but hell, this being its end by the appointment of God. No sooner, then, does the soul leave the body in mortal sin than it goes straight to hell as to its allotted place, with no other guide than the nature of sin ; and should a soul not find itself thus prevented by the justice of God, but excluded altogether from His appointment, it would endure a still greater hell — for God's appointment partakes of His mercy, and is less severe than the sin deserves ;—as it is the soul, finding no place suited to it, nor any lesser pain provided for it by God, casts itself into Hell as into its proper place. Thus, with regard to purgatory, when the soul leaves the body, and finds itself out of that state of purity in which it was created, seeing the hindrance, and that it can only be removed by purgatory, without a moment's hesitation it plunges therein ; and were there no such means provided to remove the impediment, it would forthwith beget within itself a hell worse than purgatory, because by reason of this impediment it would see itself unable to reach God, its last end : and this hindrance would be so full of pain, that, in comparison with it, purgatory, though, as I have said, it be like hell, would not be worth a thought, but be even as nothing.

CHAPTER VIII.

THE NECESSITY OF PURGATORY, AND HOW TERRIBLE IT IS.

AGAIN I say that, on God's part, I see paradise has no gate, but that whosoever will may enter therein; for God is all mercy, and stands with open arms to admit us to His glory. But still I see that the Being of God is so pure (far more than one can imagine), that should a soul see in itself even the least mote of imperfection, it would rather cast itself into a thousand hells than go with that spot into the presence of the Divine Majesty. Therefore, seeing purgatory ordained to take away such blemishes, it plunges therein, and deems it a great mercy that it can thus remove them.

No tongue can express, no mind can understand, how dreadful is purgatory. Its pain is like that of hell; and yet (as I have said) I see any soul with the least stain of imperfection accept it as a mercy, not thinking it of any moment when compared with being kept from its Love. It appears to me that the greatest pain the souls in purgatory endure proceeds from their being sensible of something in themselves displeasing to God, and that it has been done voluntarily against so much goodness; for, being in a state of grace, they know the truth, and how grievous is any obstacle which does not let them approach God.

CHAPTER IX.

THE WAY IN WHICH GOD AND THE SOULS REGARD ONE ANOTHER
IN PURGATORY—THE SAINT CONFESSES HER INABILITY TO
EXPRESS HERSELF ON THIS MATTER.

ALL the things of which I have spoken, when compared with that of which I am assured in my intelligence, so far as I am able to comprehend it in this life, are of such intensity, that, by the side of them, all things seen, all things felt, all things imagined, all things just and true, seem to me lies and things of naught. I am confounded at my inability to find stronger words. I see that God is in such perfect conformity with the soul, that when He beholds it in the purity wherein it was created by His Divine Majesty He imparts a certain attractive impulse of His burning love, enough to annihilate it, though it be immortal; and in this way so transforms the soul into Himself, its God, that it sees in itself nothing but God, who goes on thus attracting and inflaming it, until He has brought it to that state of existence whence it came forth—that is, the spotless purity wherein it was created. And when the soul, by interior illumination, perceives that God is drawing it with such loving ardour to Himself, straightway there springs up within it a corresponding fire of love for its most sweet Lord and God, which causes it wholly to melt away : it sees in the Divine light how considerately, and with what unfailing providence, God is ever leading it to

its full perfection, and that He does it all through
pure love ; it finds itself stopped by sin, and unable
to follow the heavenly attraction,—I mean that
look which God casts on it to bring it into union
with Himself : and this sense of the grievousness of
being kept from beholding the Divine light, coupled
with that instinctive longing which would fain be
without hindrance to follow the enticing look,—
these two things, I say, make up the pains of the
souls in purgatory. Not that they think any thing
of their pains, however great they be; they think
far more of the opposition they are making to the
will of God, which they see clearly is burning in-
tensely with pure love to them. God meanwhile
goes on drawing the soul to Himself by His looks
of love mightily, and, as it were, with undivided
energy : this the soul knows well; and could it find
another purgatory greater than this by which it
could sooner remove so great an obstacle, it would
immediately plunge therein, impelled by that con-
forming love which is between God and the soul.

CHAPTER X.

HOW GOD MAKES USE OF PURGATORY TO RENDER THE SOUL PER-
FECTLY PURE—THE SOUL THERE ATTAINS SUCH PURITY, THAT
WERE IT TO STAY AFTER BEING CLEANSED IT WOULD NO
LONGER SUFFER.

AGAIN, I see that the love of God directs towards
the soul certain burning rays and shafts of light,
which seem penetrating and powerful enough to an-

nihilate not merely the body, but, were it possible, the very soul itself. These work in two ways; they purify, and they annihilate.

Look at gold: the more it is melted, the better it becomes; and it could be melted so as to destroy every single defect. Such is the action of fire on material things. Now the soul cannot be annihilated so far as it is in God, but only in itself; and the more it is purified, so much the more it annihilates self, till at last it becomes quite pure and rests in God. Gold which has been purified to a certain point ceases to suffer any diminution from the action of fire, however great it be; for fire does not destroy gold, but only the dross that it may chance to have. In like manner the divine fire acts on souls: God holds them in the furnace until every defect has been burnt away, and He has brought them, each in its own degree, to a certain standard of perfection. Thus purified, they rest in God without any alloy of self; their very being is God; they become impassible because there is nothing left to be consumed. And if in this state of purity they were kept in the fire, they would feel no pain; rather it would be to them a fire of Divine Love, burning on without opposition, like the fire of life eternal.

CHAPTER XI.

THE DESIRE OF THE SOULS IN PURGATORY TO BE QUITE FREE FROM THE STAINS OF THEIR SINS—THE WISDOM OF GOD IN SUDDENLY HIDING FROM THOSE SOULS THE DEFECTS THEY HAVE.

THE soul in its creation was invested with all the conditions of which it was capable for reaching perfection, supposing it to live according to the appointment of God and keep altogether from the defilements of sin. But, marred by original sin, it loses all its gifts and graces, becomes dead; and God alone can raise it to life again. And when He has done so by baptism, still the propensity to evil remains, which, if unresisted, inclines and leads to actual sin, whereby the soul again dies. Again God restores it to life; but after this it is so tainted, so turned to self, that to recall it to its first state needs all that Divine agency that I have been speaking about, without which it never could be recalled. And when the soul finds itself on its way back to that first state, it is so enkindled with the desire of becoming one with God, that this desire becomes its purgatory; not that the soul can look at purgatory as such, but the instinct by which it is kindled, and the impediment by which it is hindered, constitute its purgatory.

God performs this last act of love without the co-operation of man; for there are so many secret imperfections within the soul, that the sight of them would drive it to despair. These are, however, all destroyed during the process I have described; and when they are consumed, God shows them to the soul, that it may understand that it was He who kindled that fire of love which consumes every imperfection there is to be consumed.

CHAPTER XII.

THE UNION OF SUFFERING AND JOY IN PURGATORY.

Know that what man deems perfection is in the sight of God a defect. All the things which have the appearance of perfection, so far as they come before the sight, the feeling, the understanding, the memory, or the will, are tainted and spoilt if not recognised as from God. For a work to be perfect, it must be wrought in us, without our co-operation as principal agents; it must be God's work, done in God, and man must not in any way take the lead. Such precisely is that operation of His pure and simple love which God finally works in us, without any merit of our own; wherein He so penetrates and burns the soul, that the surrounding body is consumed away, and can no more hold up, than one could remain alive and rest patiently amid the flames of a burning fiery furnace. It is true that the overflowing love of God bestows upon the souls in purgatory a happiness beyond expression great: but then this happiness does not in the least diminish the pain—rather the pain is constituted by this love finding itself impeded; the more perfect the love of which God makes the soul capable, the greater the pain.

In this manner the souls in purgatory at the same time experience the greatest happiness and the most excessive pain; and one does not prevent the other.

CHAPTER XIII.

HOW THE SOULS IN PURGATORY ARE NO LONGER IN A STATE TO MERIT, AND HOW THEY REGARD THE CHARITY EXERCISED IN THE WORLD FOR THEM.

IF the souls in purgatory could purge themselves of their stains by contrition, they would in a single instant discharge all their debt, so ardent and so impetuous an act would they make, seeing in so clear a light the effects of the impediment which hinders them from attaining to their end, which is God, the object of their love. And be assured that the souls have to pay what they owe even to the uttermost farthing: this is God's decree, to satisfy the demands of justice. As to the souls themselves, they have no choice of their own in the matter; they see nothing but God's will; nor do they wish things otherwise, because they have been so determined.

They would not care for alms contributed by the living to shorten their period of pain, were not those precisely balanced by the will of God; they leave all in His hands, who exacts satisfaction as it pleases His infinite goodness. And could they regard those alms apart from the Divine Will, it would be an act of selfishness which would prevent their seeing the Divine Will, and would be to them a very hell. They remain immoveably fixed on whatever God wills for them, and neither pleasure nor pain can ever again cause them to turn to self.

CHAPTER XIV. .

ON THE SUBMISSION TO THE WILL OF GOD THAT THE SOULS IN PURGATORY HAVE.

THESE souls are so closely united, so transformed into the will of God, that in all things they are satisfied with His most holy decree; and were a soul presented before God with ever so little to purge away, it would suffer grievous hurt and a torment worse than ten purgatories. That unspotted sanctity, that perfect justice, could not endure it; to do so would be unbecoming on the part of God. Should, then, the soul perceive that it lacked even a moment of satisfying God most completely, it would be to it a thing intolerable; and rather than stand thus imperfectly cleansed in the presence of God, it would plunge at once into a thousand hells.

CHAPTER XV.

HOW THE SOULS IN PURGATORY REBUKE THE MEN OF THIS WORLD.

"Would that I could cry out" (said this blessed soul, when under Divine illumination she saw these things) "loud enough to strike with fear every man upon the earth, and say, Miserable beings, why suffer ye yourselves to be so blinded by this world as to make no provision for the dire strait ye will find yourselves in at the hour of death? Ye all shelter yourselves under the hope of God's mercy, which ye say is so great; and ye consider not that this very goodness of God will rise up in judgment against you for having opposed the will of so good a Master: His mercy ought to constrain you to do all His will, and not encourage you to do evil. Be assured that His justice cannot yield, but must in one way or other be fully satisfied. Let no one buoy himself up by saying, 'I shall confess;' and then I shall receive a plenary indulgence, whereby I shall be cleansed from all my sins and get through safely.' Know that a plenary indulgence requires confession and contrition; and this latter is so difficult to obtain, that if ye knew how difficult, ye would tremble with fear, and rather make sure of not gaining than of gaining the indulgence."

CHAPTER XVI.

THE SAINT SHOWS THAT THE SUFFERINGS OF THE SOULS IN PURGATORY DO NOT DESTROY THEIR PEACE OR THEIR JOY.

I SEE that the souls in purgatory in the midst of their pains are sensible of doing two things:

First, that they are suffering willingly; for when they perceive their own deserts and God's majesty, they think that He is treating them with great leniency in afflicting them as He does; for had not goodness tempered justice with mercy through the satisfactions of the precious Blood of Jesus Christ, a thousand hells would have been the portion of a single sin through all eternity. Hence they suffer all their pains gladly, and would not rid them of a single pang, knowing that all is justly deserved and righteously ordained; they no more complain of God, so far as their will is concerned, than if they were in life eternal.

Secondly, they are conscious of feeling positive satisfaction in beholding the love and mercy with which God orders His work within them. They are made sensible of these two facts at one and the same moment, and being in a state of grace, understand them as they are, each soul according to its capacity; and they experience great happiness, which never grows less, but, on the contrary, goes on increasing the nearer they approach God. They do not know these things directly in themselves, but in God, on whom their attention is more fixed

—far more—than on the pains they suffer, and of whom in comparison they make far more account. For one glimpse of God exceeds every pain and every joy a man can conceive, and though it exceeds, does not take away one particle of the joy or of the pain.

CHAPTER XVII.

THE SAINT, IN CONCLUSION, APPLIES ALL THAT HAS BEEN SAID OF THE SOULS IN PURGATORY TO WHAT SHE FEELS AND EXPERIENCES IN HER OWN MIND.

THAT which I have thus described as going on within the souls who are actually in purgatory, I have experienced in my own soul, especially during the last two years; and each day I see and feel it more clearly. I perceive my soul in the midst of my body as in a purgatory, conformed and like to the true purgatory, in measure, however, that the body may be able to endure it and not die; yet the pain goes on increasing gradually until death. I see the soul estranged to all things, even spiritual, which can give it nourishment—as joy, delight, consolation; and it has no power of tasting any thing temporal or spiritual by will, by understanding, by memory, so that I can say, "this thing pleases me more than that other." My soul is as it were besieged in such a manner that all spiritual or bodily refreshments are gradually cut off; and when they have been cut off, the soul, although it knows well how it could have been fed and comforted by them, looks on them with feelings of hatred and abhorrence, and rejects them all without repairing its loss. This happens because there exists within the soul an impulse to get rid of every hindrance to its perfection, and that too with such severity to itself, that it would almost suffer itself to be cast into hell to reach this end: and so it goes on, removing every thing which might feed the inward man, and besieges itself so straitly, that not even the least particle of imperfection can pass without being spied out, and rejected with abhorrence. My body, too, since it can no longer communicate with the soul, is in like manner besieged, and unable to obtain any thing to refresh its human nature; there is no comfort for it but God, who does all He does to satisfy His justice lovingly and with great mercy. When I see this, I feel satisfaction and peace; but my sufferings are not the less, nor am I the less straitly besieged. No sufferings, however, could make me wish it otherwise than God has determined for me; I remain in my prison without a wish to come out till God has done all that I need. My happiness is that God should be satisfied; and the greatest pain I could endure would be being excluded from His ordinance, for I see how just and merciful it is.

I am sensible of all these things I have described as it were by sight and touch, but I cannot find fitting words to express myself as I could wish. I have said what I have, because I was conscious of its going on spiritually within me. The prison in

which I fancy myself shut up is the world; the
chain by which I am held is the body; the soul
enlightened is she who, knowing well the grievousness of being detained and kept back by any hindrance from reaching her end, suffers thereby great
pain, inasmuch as she is very tender. God, by His
grace, bestows upon her a dignity which makes her
like God, and not only like God, but even one with
Him through participating in His goodness; and
as it is impossible that God should suffer pain, so
it is with the souls that approach Him; and the
nearer they approach Him, the more they share
in that which belongs to Him. The hindrance,
then, that the soul meets with, causes it to feel an
intolerable pain; and the pain, together with the
hindrance, obstruct those properties which it has
by nature, and which by grace are revealed to it;
and not being able to attain them, although capable
of them, the soul remains in suffering great in proportion to its appreciation of God. This appreciation of God grows with its knowledge of God;
and its knowledge is greater the more it is free
from sin; and the delay becomes more and more
terrible, because the soul, wholly immersed in God,
knows Him without error, there being nothing in
the way to prevent such knowledge. The man
who would die sooner than offend God, feels death
and the pain of dying; but the sight of God sup-
plies him with a zeal which makes him think more
of the divine honour than bodily death. In like
manner, a soul knowing what God has appointed

for it thinks more of the appointment than any
outward or inward pain, no matter how dreadful;
and this because God, the author of it, surpasses
every thing that can be thought of or imagined.
The participation of Himself that God grants the
soul, however slight it be, keeps it so wholly
taken up with His majesty that it can think of
nothing else : every thing to do with self passes
away,—it neither sees, speaks, nor knows loss or
pain of its own ; but all this, as has been already
clearly said, it perceives at the instant of passing
from this life. Finally, in conclusion, I mean that
God, who is good and great, destroys all which is
of man, and purgatory purifies it.

APPENDICES.

—◆—

Appendix A.

The Saint must here be understood to mean that the souls
in purgatory cannot recollect the *specific* reasons of the pains
they suffer; that they cannot say, "I have done such and
such sins, for which I deserve to be here." She cannot mean
absolutely that they do not know that the pains they suffer
are in punishment for their sins. For besides such ignorance
being scarcely conceivable, it is contrary to her own express
statement in chap. vii., where she says, "that that which
causes the souls in purgatory most pain is the seeing in
themselves a thing displeasing to God; and the being conscious that it has been admitted against so much goodness."

Appendix B.

There is a difference of opinion among theologians as to the
nature of that purification which the souls undergo in purgatory.   From what are they purified? from the guilt of sin,
or simply from imperfections? If from imperfections, in
what sense do they become perfect? In that they are in-
trinsically improved; or is it merely that they have bettered
their condition before God?

Bellarmine goes so far as to maintain that the *culpa* or
guilt of venial sin is remitted in purgatory. To Calvin's
objection to Matt. xii. 32 being quoted in favour of purgatory, because there our Lord is speaking of sin being
remitted in the world to come *quoad culpam*, whereas purgatory only remits sin *quoad pœnam*, he replies, "that at
least venial sin is remitted in purgatory *quoad culpam*"
(De Purg. lib. i. c. iv. 6). He says that the true opinion is
St. Thomas's, that the guilt of venial sin, *culpas veniales*, is
remitted in purgatory by an act of love and patient endurance
(De Purg. lib. i. c. xiv. 22).

Suarez, on the other hand, does not seem to admit that
purgatory betters the soul in any other sense than enabling
it to discharge the debt of punishment due to sin (Suarez,
Disp. xi. sec. iv. a 2, § 10). All the guilt of sin, he says, is
remitted at the first moment of the soul's separation from the
body,—*in primo instanti separationis animæ a corpore*,—"By

D

a single act of contrition, whereby the will is wholly converted to God and turned away from every venial sin" (§13). And *in this way*, he says, sin may be remitted—*quoad culpam*—in purgatory, because the soul's purification dates from this moment (§ 10). As to bad habits and vicious inclinations, he says, " we ought not *to* imagine that the soul is detained for these : for so far as they arise from the sensitive appetite, they are laid aside with the body ; so far as they are in the will, they are either taken away at the moment of death, or expelled by an infusion of the contrary virtues when the soul enters into glory" (Disp. xlvii. sec. i. 6).

Now which view, it may be asked, does St. Catherine countenance in the present treatise,—that of Bellarmine or that of Suarez?   She is plainly unfavourable to Bellarmine's view of the *culpa*, or guilt of venial sin, being remitted in purgatory : for she says (chap. iii.) "that the souls in purgatory are free from the guilt of sin, and nothing is between God and them except the punishment;" and in chap. iv., that the souls in purgatory have only the punishment, the guilt —*la colpa*—having been cancelled at the moment of death; and so far she supports Suarez.   Yet there are not wauting many passages which make it very doubtful whether she is altogether on his side.

What does the Saint understand by the *macchia*, or stain, which she says is upon the soul after sin, and to get rid of which it must needs go through purgatory?   According to St. Thomas, the effect of sin is threefold : 1. It weakens the soul's natural propensity to good—*corrumpit bonum naturæ;* 2. It leaves a stain—*causat maculam*—on the soul; 3. It incurs a debt of punishment—*facit hominem reum pœnæ.* The stain, or *macula*, is altogether a privative idea.   As the result of mortal sin, " it is that shadow which is upon the soul when the light of grace can no longer shine there, which shade in some way or other takes its shape* from the actual sin which has caused it,—*Est privatio nitoris gratiæ seu quod idem est ipsiusmet gratiæ connotans peccatum actuale præcedens a quo causatur*" (Billuart, vol. iv. d. vii. a. 11).   As the result of venial sin, it is the diminution of the fervour of charity : *Est privatio fervoris charitatis ex peccatis actualibus venialibus* (Ibid.).

Speaking analogously of the souls in purgatory, does the Saint mean by the *macchia*, or stain, that shade or gloom which is over the soul in consequence of being deprived of the light of glory?

The comparison in chapter ii. at first sight seems fa-

---

* " Sicut umbra quæ est varia pro diversitate corporum." (St. Thomas, Sum. Th. I. 2, q. 86.)

vourable to such a notion; but then it is to be observed in that comparison, that the Saint has evidently before her mind the *ruggine del peccato* as the cause, not the effect, of God's not shining into the soul.

Perhaps, then, there is no reference in this *macchia* to St. Thomas's *macula*. It may simply mean the state of the soul which has not paid the debt of punishment when it ought. For that it includes in it the idea of an imperfection in the soul, and not simple punishment, seems evidently implied by its being opposed (chap. viii.) not merely to God's justice, but to His purity. But does it not also include the *corruptio naturalis boni*,—that weakness in the direction of virtue, those bad dispositions, those unheavenly tastes, which the soul contracts through sin, and which remain after the guilt of sin is remitted? Certainly such could be got rid of, as Suarez suggests, in a moment; but there seems a moral fitness that it should not be so,—that as they have been gained by slow degrees, and a repetition of acts, they should be got rid of by a like process,—that in getting back to virtue, we should have to retrace the steps we have taken in departing therefrom. We know that such is God's way of dealing with souls in this life, why should we think it is different in purgatory?

There are several passages in the treatise which make one think that this must have been St. Catherine's view. In chapter xi. she almost, if not quite, says so. She says that when the soul has been restored to grace, it often remains so *stained and turned to self* (*imbrattata e conversa verso se stessa*), that to recall it to its first state, as God created it, needs all those operations of the Divine power which she has been describing, without which it could never be recalled. Now what can she mean here but selfish habits? She concludes the treatise by saying, that " God, who is great and good, destroys all that is of man, and purgatory purifies it." Now what can be meant by *all that is of man* except earthly inclinations?

It is very easy to reconcile what the Saint says elsewhere, which looks the other way. For instance, in chapter iii., where she says, that there is nothing between God and the souls except the punishment, it may be conceived that the Saint includes this very getting rid of the bad inclinations as a part of the punishment : observe, in connection with the preceding context, what she says in chapter xi. about the *istinto acceso ed impedito* constituting the soul's purgatory. Again, it may be thought that in chapter i. the idea of imperfection is excluded from the souls in purgatory; but the Saint there only speaks of the impossibility of acts of imperfection existing in purgatory: such inclinations and habits as are here supposed are altogether passive. And that she does not exclude all idea of imperfection is evident both, as was said before, from her making the impediment something opposed to God's purity, and from her own express statement in chapter xi., where she says " that, there are so many secret imperfections in the soul, that were it to see them it would be driven to despair; that God in that final condition of the soul consumes them, and when consumed, shows them to the soul, that it may know that it is He who has caused the fire of love, which consumes whatever of imperfection there is to consume."

Bellarmine, an authority on such a subject by no means inferior to Suarez, doubts, " An sicut in hâc vitâ immoderatus amor erga temporalia purgatur a Deo variis afflictionibus, ut mortibus uxoris, liberorum, &c., ita etiam credibile sit, post hanc vitam adhuc remanere in animâ separatâ aliquas reliquias talium affectionum actualium quæ purgari debeant tribulationibus et molestiis" (De Pur. lib. i. c. xv. 25).

On the whole, there does not appear any thing contrary to sound theology in the idea of such an intrinsic improvement taking place in the soul in purgatory as is implied in the gradual getting rid of passive bad habits and earthly tastes. Such a notion is very much in accordance with what we know of God's dealings with the soul here on earth, and seems countenanced by the present treatise.